WE ARE ALL IN THE DUMPS

WITH
JACK AND GUY

WE ARE ALL IN THE DUMPS
WITH JACK AND GUY

BY
MAURICE SENDAK

Michael di Capua Books

HarperCollins Publishers

FOR DIAMONDS ARE TRUMPS

THE MOON'S IN A FIT

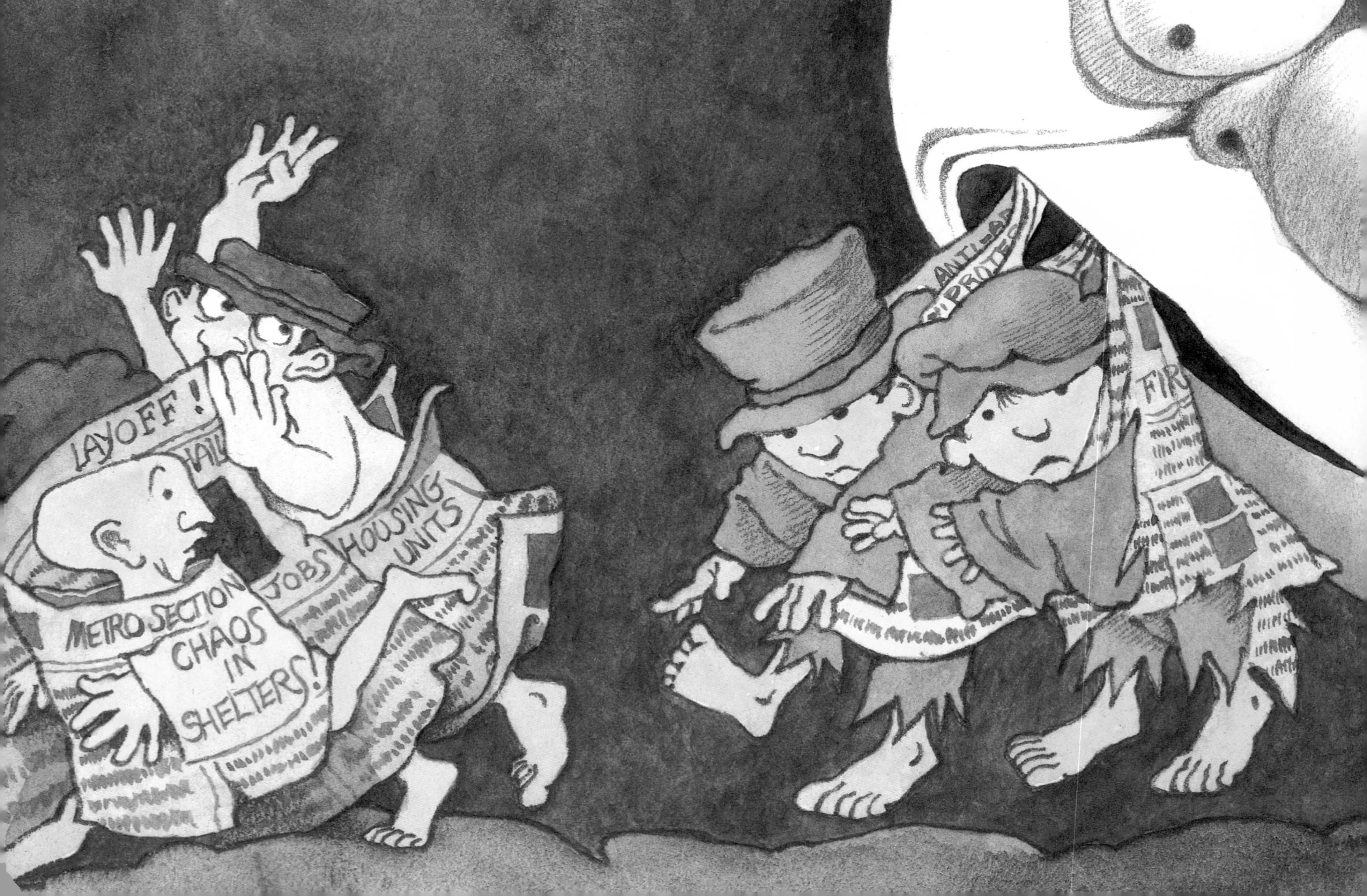

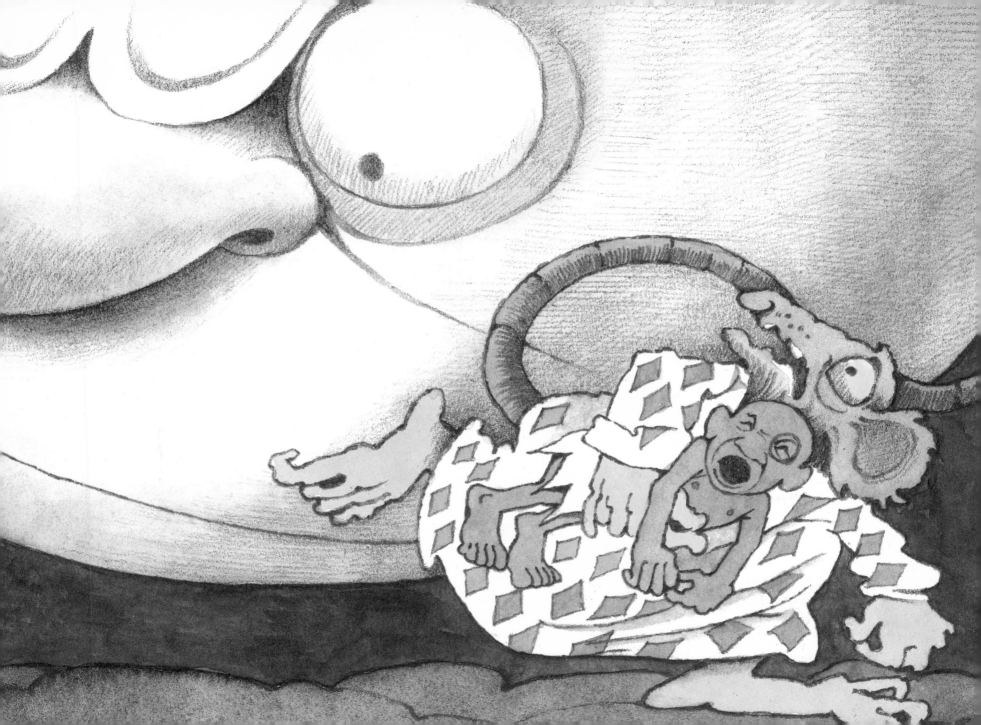

AND THE HOUSES ARE BUILT

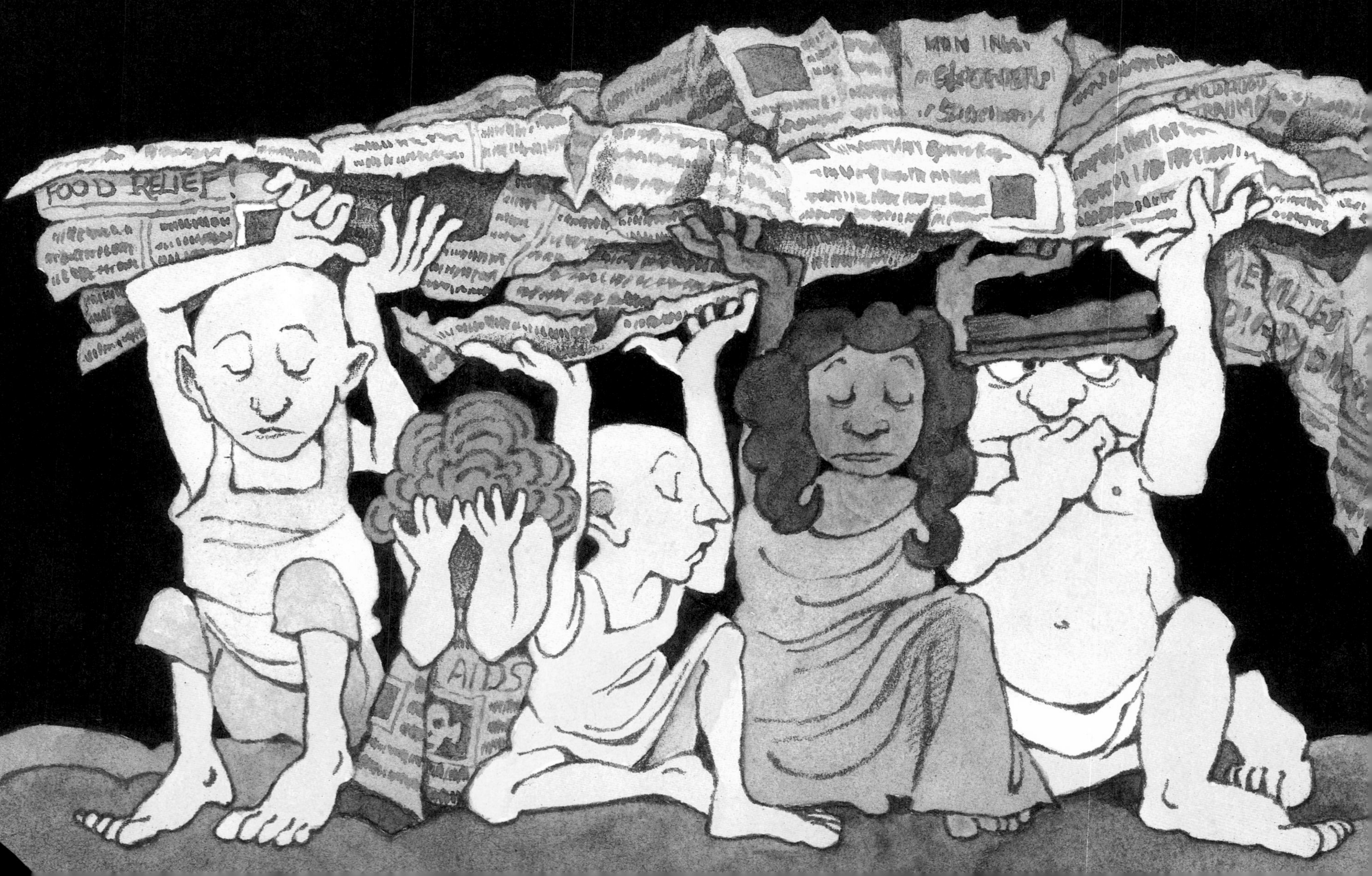

JACK AND GUY

WENT OUT IN THE RYE

AND THEY FOUND A LITTLE BOY

WITH ONE BLACK EYE

COME SAYS JACK LET'S KNOCK HIM

ON THE HEAD

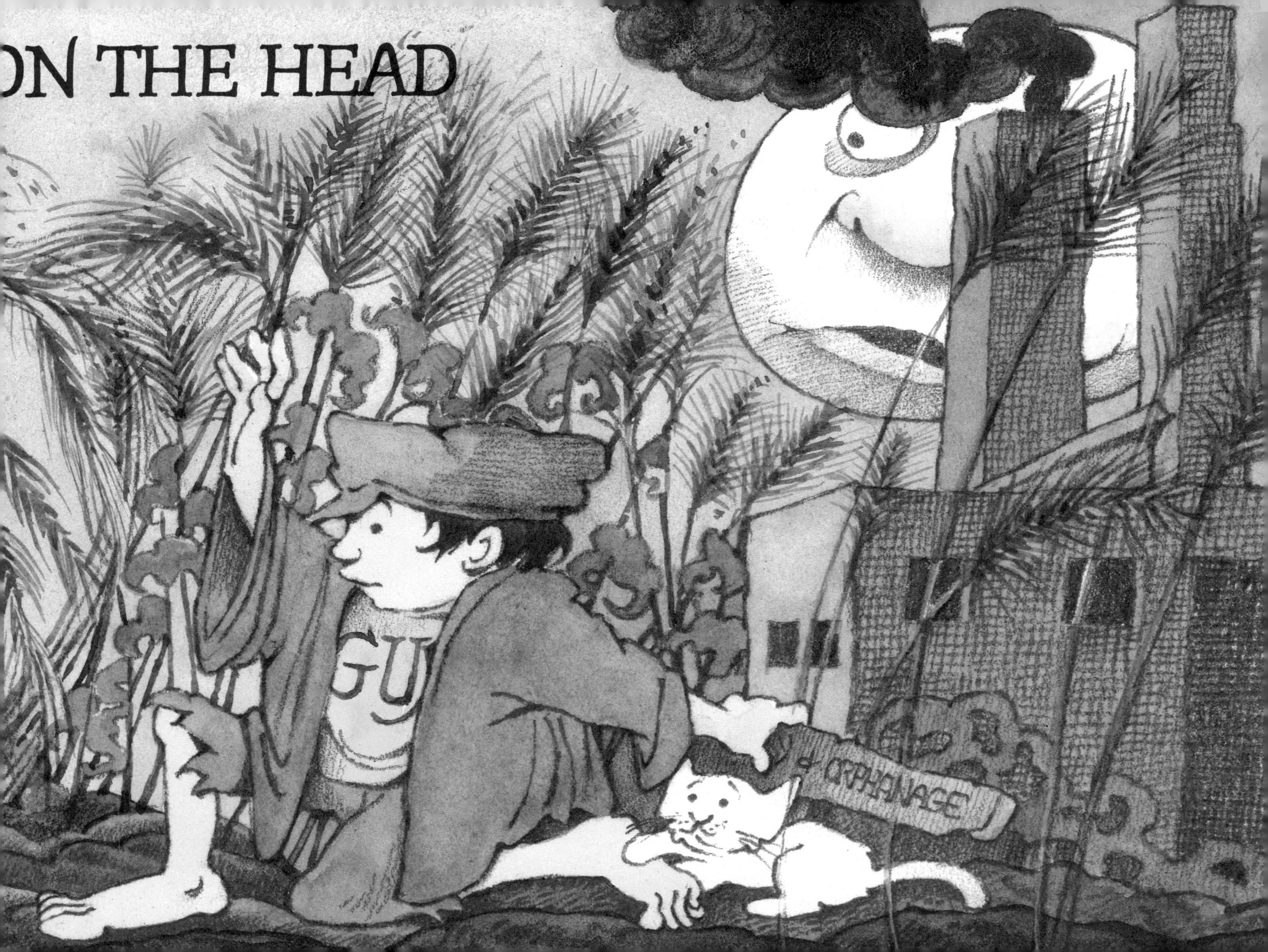

NO SAYS GUY

LET'S BUY HIM SOME BREAD

ST. PAUL'S BAKERY

YOU BUY ONE LOAF

AND I'LL BUY TWO

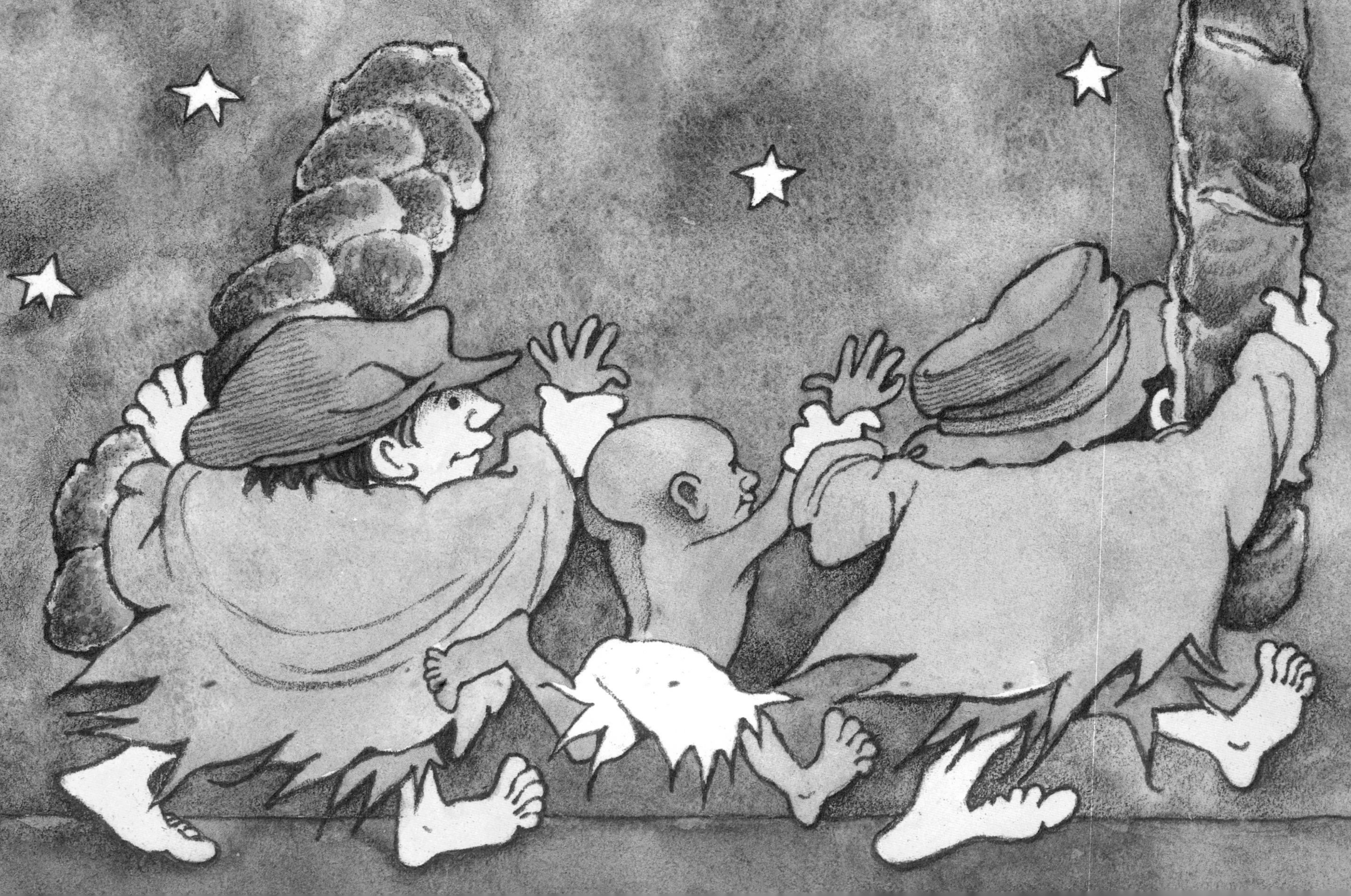

AND WE'LL BRING HIM UP

AS OTHER FOLK DO